The Night Before
Summer Camp

By Natasha Wing · Illustrated by Mindy Pierce

Grosset & Dunlap

'Twas the night before day camp
when at the town park
the counselors were working
till well after dark.

The canoes were moored
by the boat dock with care,
in hopes that young paddlers
soon would be there.

The children were nestled
all snug in their beds
while visions of butterflies
danced in their heads.

But not everyone was happy
about going to camp . . .
especially Rick,
who was the worry-bird champ.

In the morning Mom woke him.
"Rise and shine, kiddo!"
But he pulled up the covers.
"I don't want to go.

"I don't know anyone there.
I'll be gone all day.
Can't I just go over
to Tommy's and play?"

"Camp is one giant playtime,"
Mom said, "so don't you stress.
And it's not an overnighter."

"Okay. I'll try it, I guess."

The bus picked him up
at the end of the street

and dropped off the kids
where the sign said to meet.

There was a whole bunch of children—
none that Rick knew.
He felt lost and lonely.
"What do I do?"

"Come join the Lion's Cubs!"
said his counselor Kim,
who today was teaching
the kids how to swim.

"Kick your feet! Move your arms!
Place your face in the water!
Excellent, Rick!
You swim like an otter!"

For the rest of the morning,
the Cubs explored nature trails.

They saw butterflies, birds,
crawly bugs, snakes, and snails.

They gathered up sticks
and found bark to make boats.
Then set them a'sail—

"Hey, look! Mine really floats!"

When what at the edge of the lake should appear,
but a beautiful doe and two baby brown deer.

Their eyes—how they twinkled! Their bobtails so twitchy!
Their legs were so slender, while Rick's were so itchy!

"Anybody starving?" asked Kim.
"It's time to eat lunch!"

But Rick wasn't hungry.
He missed his mom a whole bunch.

Counselor Kim sat beside him
and asked, "Are you okay?"
"I want to go home," Rick told her.
"I'm kind of nervous today."

Kim smiled and said, "Hey, little Cub.
I'm nervous, just like you.
This is my very first job.
I'm away from home, too.

"Last night I tossed
and turned in my bed.
I couldn't get the
jitters out of my head!"

"Same here!" replied Rick.
"I really understand!
So whenever you're nervous,
just hold on to my hand."

"It's a deal!" said Kim.
"And thanks for the talk.
Could you help me carry
the jump rope and chalk?"

For the rest of the week,
Rick had oodles of fun!

There were three-legged races,
which he and Kim won!

He made a scrapbook and drum
at the arts and crafts table.

starred in a play
from an old Aesop's fable.

Day camp ended on Friday—
oh what a bummer!

"I want to go back
for *two* weeks next summer!"